This book belongs to

Norbett Bear, MD

Paul Carson is a practising medical doctor who lives in Dublin with his wife and two children. He is the author of four other books on health problems in children. *Norbett Bear, MD* is his first children's book.

Norbett Bear, MD

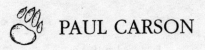 PAUL CARSON

Published in 1994 by
Poolbeg,
A division of Poolbeg Enterprises Ltd,
Knocksedan House,
123 Baldoyle Industrial Estate,
Dublin 13, Ireland

A catalogue record for this book is available from the British Library.

ISBN 1 85371 409 7

Illustrated by Donald Teskey
Cover design by Poolbeg Group Services Ltd
Set by Poolbeg Group Services Ltd in Stone 13/18
Printed by The Guernsey Press Company Ltd,
Vale, Guernsey, Channel Islands.

*For Jean, Emily and David
and special thanks to Norbett and
Bamber bears for allowing me to
share their adventures*

Contents

1

Norbett Makes
an Announcement

Norbett Bear was a very impatient bear. "Bamber . . . are you in there? Open this door at once!"

He had only knocked twice on Bamber Bear's cave door, but when Bamber didn't answer quickly enough, Norbett began to shout through the letterbox. "Bamber . . . are you in or are you not?"

Norbett was a tall, slim, well-dressed bear who wore red braces and brightly coloured bow ties.

"Bamber . . . will you open this door! I have something very important to tell you."

When he was in a hurry, nothing stood in his way.

Inside the cave Bamber was staring gloomily at his own reflection in the mirror. He was a small bear with a large appetite and a weight problem. His ample tummy bulged over his trousers and there was a hole in the sleeve of his yellow sweater where an elbow had burst through. The letterbox on the door flipped open and Norbett's eyes peered through.

"BAMBER BEAR . . . ARE YOU IN OR DO I HAVE TO BREAK THIS DOOR DOWN TO FIND OUT!" he roared. A most impatient bear was Norbett.

Bamber sighed deeply and padded over to the door. He knew by the way Norbett was carrying on there was going to be no peace until he was let in.

"Who wants to know?" he shouted.

"Me," growled Norbett, watching every move through the opening.

"Who's me?" asked Bamber.

"Who do you think 'Me' is? It's Norbett. That's who it is. Who else would call on you?"

Bamber made a face at the door. "I have other friends, you know. You're not the only one to call on me."

Norbett pounded the door again. "Bamber, will you open the door! I have very important news for you."

"Oh," said Bamber, fiddling with the bolt on the door, "is this important news good or important news bad?"

Norbett watched Bamber at the lock.

"Pull the bolt, don't push it." With a loud rattle Bamber unlocked the cave door and Norbett burst inside.

"Bamber!" he exclaimed, "sometimes your bumbling reaches new heights!"

"Is that a good thing or a bad thing?" asked Bamber innocently.

"No it is not a good thing," snorted Norbett. "Bears are smart, bright and intelligent animals. But some of us . . . " and here he gave Bamber a long hard stare, "some of us do a very good impersonation of being dense." He snapped his braces against his chest and pushed the door closed.

"However," he continued, "I haven't all day to prattle. Do you want to hear my news or not?"

"Is it good news or bad news?" asked Bamber carefully.

"GOOD NEWS, BAMBER," boomed Norbett. "GOOD NEWS INDEED. IN FACT, VERY GOOD NEWS."

"Okay," said Bamber wearily. "Tell me. Good news I can take. Bad news I can do without."

"But this is excellent news, Bamber," added Norbett enthusiastically, and he strode around the cave, snapping his braces. "It is more than just good news, it is excellent news. You will be so pleased when you hear it."

"I am pleased enough already," sighed Bamber, "so get on with it."

Norbett stopped in the middle of the cave and put on his Important-Looking Face. He held a paw up for silence.

"Bamber bear," he announced grandly.

"Yes, Norbett?" said Bamber.

"Quiet!" snapped Norbett. "Don't interrupt!"

Bamber made a face behind his paw and pretended to listen attentively.

"Bamber bear," continued Norbett, "I wish to announce the opening of the first Forest Medical Centre."

"The wha . . . ?" Bamber butted in.

Norbett gave him a withering look. "The first Forest Medical Centre," he said. "You are now looking at the first director of this same centre. Meet Dr Norbett Bear, MD." He thrust out a paw towards Bamber and shook his paw firmly. Bamber's mouth opened and closed but nothing came out.

"Well," growled Norbett, "say something."

"I am pleased," croaked Bamber finally.

"Good," said Norbett grandly. "I thought you would be."

"But," said Bamber thoughtfully, "what do you know about being a doctor?"

"Nothing," exclaimed Norbett. "N-O-T-H-I-N-G. Nothing at all! But I've been *reading* all about it and there's not much to it. You just have to *act* like a doctor and nobody will know any different. I've been working on the acting bit and now I am quite ready to start administering to the animals of this forest. They'll come flocking as soon as they hear all about me."

Bamber thought this all over very carefully. "Norbett Bear, MD?" he mused out loud. "What does the MD stand for?"

"Mighty Doctor," replied Norbett, inspecting his claws closely. "Or Marvellous Doctor . . . or even Magnificent Doctor. I haven't worked that one out yet. But all doctors have MD after their names so I suppose it must mean something."

"And when will you begin?"

"Today," said Norbett. "Today. And that's why I've called on you. I have come to interview you for the position of First Assistant."

"First Assistant?" exclaimed Bamber. "First Assistant to whom?"

"First Assistant to me," snapped Norbett, his eyes raised to heaven.

"First Assistant!" gasped Bamber. "First Assistant to Dr Norbett Bear, MD?"

"Yes," said Norbett. "I thought I would interview you first for this important position."

Bamber marched around the cave, his chest puffed out. "Bamber Bear, First Assistant to Dr Norbett Bear," he muttered.

"MD," corrected Norbett. "Don't forget

the MD bit."

"Yes," said Bamber, nodding in agreement. "Dr Norbett Bear, MD."

"That's better," said Norbett smugly.

"First Assistant to Dr Norbett Bear, MD," whispered Bamber to the mirror. "Bamber Bear . . . First Assistant. I rather like the sound of that. I could live with that."

"I thought you would be pleased," said Norbett.

"When can I start?" asked Bamber, full of himself at the thought of a new position in life.

"As soon as you have been trained," replied Norbett. "There will be an intensive training exercise to begin with and if you come through that successfully, then, and only then . . . " he warned severely, " . . . will you be confirmed as my First Assistant."

"Have no fear," said Bamber, still looking at himself in the mirror. He pulled in his stomach to make a better impression. "There will be no better First Assistant in all the valley."

"Attaboy, Bamber," said Norbett.

"The first assisting I will do will make all other First Assistants ashamed to think they had ever thought of first assisting."

"Right on, Bamber," cheered Norbett.

"In years to come, the forest animals will talk in hushed voices about Bamber Bear, First Assistant, and his exploits."

"Okay . . . okay," growled Norbett. "Knock it off, knock it off. You've got the job. Just stop rabbiting on about it will you?"

"You know it makes sense," said Bamber smugly and he waved at himself in the mirror. "Good-bye Bamber Bear, a nobody bear. Hello Bamber Bear, First Assistant to the famous Dr Norbett Bear, MD."

Norbett groaned as he opened the cave door. "I hope I've made the right choice here," he muttered under his breath. "Come on, First Assistant, let's get going. We have a lot of work to do."

So Dr Norbett Bear, MD, and his newly appointed First Assistant strode out into the forest to begin their new lives together.

2

Bamber Bear, FA

Through the forest went Bamber and Norbett bears, Norbett striding ahead humming to himself and Bamber following behind as fast as his legs would carry, muttering all the while, "Bamber Bear, First Assistant . . . Bamber Bear, First Assistant."

At the edge of the forest, in another clearing beside a large pine tree, stands Norbett Bear's cave and here he and Bamber sat down to plan their next move.

"First of all," began Norbett, "we will have an intensive training exercise."

"Great," said Bamber, all enthusiastic.

"Now I am going outside," continued Norbett, "and when I return I am going to be an Awkward Patient."

"A what?" gasped Bamber.

"An Awkward Patient," replied Norbett. "You know the sort. Someone who thinks he knows everything. Someone who thinks he knows more than the doctor and who only goes to see if the doctor is as good as him. A real dumbo." He placed a paw on Bamber's shoulder. "Now what is he?"

"A real dumbo!" shouted Bamber enthusiastically.

"Right on, Bamber, right on," cheered Norbett.

Bamber smiled broadly. He was beginning to enjoy this training exercise already.

"When I return, you pretend to be the doctor and I will be the patient," added Norbett. He marched out of the cave and waited for a moment. Inside Bamber composed himself.

"Knock, knock, knock," went the door

and in came Norbett, snapping his braces against his chest.

"Good morning doctor," he said.

"Good morning, dumbo," replied Bamber.

"WHAT DO YOU MEAN, DUMBO!" roared Norbett. "WHO ARE YOU CALLING A DUMBO?"

"Bbbuutt . . . " stammered Bamber, "you said you were going to be an Awkward Patient and you said they were all dumbos."

"Yes," growled Norbett angrily, "but you don't go around calling them that to their faces."

"Oh," said Bamber timidly, "don't I?"

"No, you don't," growled Norbett. "And," he continued, "you are supposed to give them a chance to tell you what's wrong with them before you start insulting them!"

"Righto," agreed Bamber, mopping his brow in the face of this onslaught.

"Now," said Norbett severely, "let's try again. Remember, I am going to be an

Awkward Patient and you had better be very careful how you deal with me."

"Righto," said Bamber, trying to look composed.

"And remember no calling me names this time," warned Norbett.

"Never," vowed Bamber.

Out went Norbett once more, snapping his braces and snorting. He stood at the cave door until he had counted to fifty and then marched back inside. He smiled at Bamber and Bamber smiled weakly back.

"Good morning, doctor," said Norbett.

"Good morning, Awkward Patient," replied Bamber sweetly.

"WHAT DO YOU MEAN, AWKWARD PATIENT!" roared Norbett. "WHO DO YOU THINK YOU'RE CALLING AN AWKWARD PATIENT?"

Bamber's heart nearly stopped.

"Bbbuutt . . . " he stammered through chattering teeth. "I thought you said you were an Awkward Patient this time."

"I know I said I was going to be an

awkward patient, but I don't want you going round calling me that to my face!"

Bamber wanted to run but couldn't get past the cave door so he just sat tight in his chair and trembled.

Norbett took deep breaths in and out through his nose, trying to calm down. He counted up to one hundred before speaking again.

"Bamber," he said finally, through gritted teeth.

"Yes, Norbett," replied Bamber, hardly daring to look.

"Bamber," continued Norbett, "this time I want you to go outside and I will stay inside and show you how a *real* doctor handles the situation."

"Do I have to play at being an Awkward Patient?" asked Bamber hesitantly.

"No, Bamber," Norbett replied with a forced smile, "just be yourself. That's quite enough for me at the moment."

Bamber was only too delighted to breathe clear air outside the cave again and he leaned against the wall, wiping his brow.

"You can come in now," shouted Norbett from inside.

"Just a minute," Bamber shouted back. "I'm preparing myself."

"No need to, Bamber," shouted Norbett again. "You'll be fine the way you are."

Bamber looked up to heaven and offered a silent prayer. He took a deep breath, let it out slowly and walked back into the cave with a rather weak smile on his face.

"Good morning, doctor," he said.

"Good morning, Bamber Bear," replied Norbett, all sweetness and light. "And what seems to be the matter with you?"

"I've got a bad back," said Bamber, stooping slightly for effect. "I have this terrible pain going up my back, into my neck, down my arm, into my paw, up the other paw, up the other arm, around my head, into my eyes, through my nose, out my mouth and on to the tip of my tongue!"

"Wha . . . ?" growled Norbett in amazement.

"I have this bad back with pains shooting up and d . . . " began Bamber again.

"I HEARD ALL THAT!" roared Norbett at the top of his voice. "I heard all about your miserable pains. When did you start to get bad backs and hyperactive pains, then?"

"I'm only pretending," Bamber growled back angrily. "If I'm supposed to be a patient, then I need to have something wrong with me, don't I?"

"*Something*, maybe," Norbett snapped. "Something simple, maybe. Not a hundred-miles-an-hour-pain that's going to take days to sort out!"

Bamber pouted and said nothing.

"Anyway," continued Norbett angrily, "I'm not ready for bad backs yet. I haven't read the books on backs yet. Why couldn't you have something simple like the flu or a head cold or ingrown toenails or something like that?"

"Because I don't have the flu or a head cold or ingrown toenails," Bamber complained bitterly. "And anyway," he continued, "what sort of a doctor are you going to be if you only deal with the things you think you've read up about, huh? What sort of a doctor tells all the patients in his waiting-room that he isn't ready for bad backs yet and that he's only going to deal with colds, the flu and ingrown toenails, huh?"

Norbett looked embarrassed and muttered something Bamber couldn't hear.

Bamber put on his Terribly Fed-Up face and moved towards the cave door.

"Anyway," he added, "I'm fed up with all the abuse I have to take. I think I'll go home. I don't think I want to be a First Assistant."

"You don't get to wear the special First Assistant uniform then," said Norbett suddenly.

Bamber stopped in his tracks. "Special uniform?" he exclaimed. "You didn't tell me there was a special uniform."

Norbett stood up and went into a back room of the cave, returning with two coats, one white and the other yellow. He pulled the white coat on himself and fastened the buttons at the front. Then he turned around so that Bamber could see the writing on the back:

Dr Norbett Bear, MD
Surgeon . . . Doctor . . . All-round
Medical Handyman
Reasonable Fees

"Well what do you think? Pretty nifty, eh?" said Norbett. Bamber was deeply impressed.

"Very impressive indeed," he replied.

Norbett then held up the yellow coat and turned it so that Bamber could read the writing on the back:

Bamber Bear FA
First Assistant to Dr Norbett Bear, MD
Accounts Payable Here
(Please do not ask for credit
as a refusal often offends)

"Well what do you think? Pretty nifty, eh?"

Bamber was thrilled with the coat and slipped it on very carefully. He looked around and found a long mirror in the corner and stood admiring himself.

Turning this way and that, he craned his neck to read the writing on the back. Then he strutted around the cave muttering, "First Assistant . . . Bamber Bear, First Assistant to the famous Dr Norbett Bear, MD." He paused in front of the mirror again and spoke to his reflection. "Good morning, Mr Patient, can I be of assistance to you? Would you like some help?"

"Attaboy, Bamber," cheered Norbett as he watched.

"Perhaps you wish to make a special appointment with the maestro?" continued Bamber, warming to his role.

"Brilliant!" Norbett roared his approval.

"Oh you don't have an appointment . . . tut tut. I'm not sure we can fit you in this year at all. Norbett Bear, MD is a very busy bear."

"Superb, Bamber. Superb!" roared Norbett, sitting down at the table to watch. "Don't give him an appointment for five years . . . if he thinks he can wander in here and expect to be cured at a moment's notice, he has another thought coming."

"I'm very sorry," said Bamber to the mirror. "I believe the doctor is operating at present . . . a very delicate problem and I really can't disturb him."

"Fantastic! Fantastic, absolutely fantastic," cheered Norbett, standing up and clapping. "I knew you would make an excellent First Assistant."

Bamber bowed. "When do I begin my official first assisting, Norbett?" he asked. "I feel I am quite ready for the job."

"Right away, Bamber, right away," said Norbett. "Just help me put this board up outside and we're ready to start."

At the back of the cave lay a large two-sided board Norbett had prepared. He and Bamber carried it outside. They looked for a suitable position and finally decided to leave it close enough to the door so that all the animals would know to go inside as soon as they saw it. Bamber read out the writing on the board:

FOREST MEDICAL CENTRE
Medical Director: Dr Norbett Bear, MD
First Assistant: Bamber Bear, FA
Pains Eased . . . Aches Relieved
. . . Sickness Cured
No Job Too Small . . . Commissions Taken
Don't Delay – Make An Appointment
Today

"Oh very good, Norbett," he enthused,

"very good indeed."

"Now you stand nearby and render assistance as soon as you see anyone as much as looking at the board," ordered Norbett.

"Leave it to me, doctor," said Bamber confidently.

"Attaboy, Bamber," said Norbett, "I'll be just inside, brushing up on my surgical skills if you need me."

Bamber stood beside the sign for ages but no one came through the clearing. He marched up and down, discussing appointments with imaginary patients, warning them to turn up in time and not to be bringing all their relations and friends and crowding the place out. He was so engrossed in his thoughts that he almost missed the horse who trotted quietly out of the forest up to the board and began to read.

"Good morning horse," said Bamber as soon as he saw him.

"Good morning bear," replied the horse. "I didn't know there was a doctor here."

"Not feeling too well then?" asked Bamber hopefully.

"Never felt better," replied the horse, shaking his mane in the air. "Never felt better in all my life."

"Not even a bit of colic . . . or scurf . . . or even a small attack of galloping footrot?" pressed Bamber, anxious for business.

"Not a bit," said the horse, scratching his snout against the board.

"What a pity," muttered Bamber under his breath.

"I beg your pardon," snorted the horse. "What was that?"

"Nothing . . . nothing," replied Bamber trying not to look too disappointed. "Nothing at all."

Inside the cave Norbett heard the voices and came out to investigate.

"Good morning horse," he said with a broad smile. "Is my assistant helping you?"

"Who are you?" asked the horse loftily.

"That's Norbett," interrupted Bamber,

proudly.

"Doctor Norbett to you, First Assistant," sniffed Norbett.

"Sorry," said Bamber. "Doctor Norbett."

"MD," whispered Norbett behind a paw. "Don't forget the MD bit."

"Sorry again," muttered Bamber. "Doctor Norbett Bear . . . MD."

"Humph!" neighed the horse, wondering what the two were going on about. "Your friend here," and he nodded towards Bamber, "was asking how I felt."

"Excellent, First Assistant, excellent," said Norbett and he patted Bamber on the head.

Bamber put on his Very Pleased Face.

"And how do you feel?" pressed Norbett.

"Never better . . . never better," replied the horse grandly.

Norbett gave the horse a long, hard look. "Hmmmm," he said, "you don't look very well."

"I've never felt better in all my life," snorted the horse again in disgust. "In fact, I was just out for my morning canter and remarking to myself how well I felt when I stumbled into this clearing."

"Oh-ho," said Norbett, shaking his head, "that's a very bad sign."

"What's a very bad sign?" asked the horse suspiciously.

"Feeling so well," replied Norbett. "Always a bad sign in a horse." He stood beside the horse and examined his eyes carefully. "Open your mouth," he ordered and the horse obliged. "Tut-tut," went Norbett with a sad shake of his head. "This is the worst case of good health I have ever seen," he added. "A definite form of *Rudicus Goodicus Healthicus*."

"What?" exclaimed the horse, breaking out in a sweat. Even Bamber looked amazed and stood with his mouth open.

"*Rudicus Goodicus Healthicus*," repeated Norbett solemnly. "A very dangerous form of good health, especially in horses."

"Is it serious?" asked the horse, now in a state of panic.

"Only if you're a horse," replied Norbett

casually.

"BUT I AM A HORSE!" roared the horse, pawing the ground with his forelegs.

"So you are . . . so you are," gasped Norbett in mock horror. Bamber was beginning to feel a bit worried by now.

"What should I do?" asked the horse anxiously.

"Wait here," ordered Norbett and he rushed back inside his cave. He pulled open a cupboard and scrambled through it until he found exactly what he wanted. With a fiendish grin he shook the bottle vigorously and then peeled off the outer label. "Gulp this down as fast as you can,"

he said as soon as he was outside again. "Quickly, before it's too late."

The horse couldn't get the liquid into himself fast enough. With one long, glug-glug-glug, he polished off the brown mixture and pulled a face of pure disgust at the end. Then he snorted and reared up on his hind legs, letting out a loud neigh. "I feel better already!" he exclaimed.

"Attaboy horse," cheered Norbett as he watched. "Attaboy!"

The horse cantered around the clearing, snorting and neighing and shaking his mane in the air. He cleared a couple of fallen branches for good measure, finally disappearing into the forest shouting his thanks to the heavens for the miraculous cure.

Bamber looked on in amazement. "What did you give him?" he asked.

Norbett started to laugh. He bent over double, holding his sides, tears streaming down his face.

"Come on," complained Bamber. "What exactly did you give him in that bottle?"

"HORSE RADISH SAUCE!" roared Norbett in between peals of laughter. "Horse Radish Sauce! Get it? Horse Radish Sauce!"

Bamber groaned. He continued to groan the whole way home at the end of the day, long after Norbett had finished with all his training exercises. Indeed Bamber's head was spinning as he climbed into bed that night.

"I do hope Norbett has no more training exercises or funny cures tomorrow," he thought as he turned out the light and fell asleep.

Back in his own cave Norbett Bear, doctor, surgeon and general medical handyman, was planning his next moves. He grinned from ear to ear as he wrote them down so as not to forget.

3

Bamber Tries to Fly

"I have plans for you today," announced Norbett to Bamber the next morning.

Bamber groaned. He had turned up early, just like he reckoned a good First Assistant would, and was very keen to get on with assisting. But he knew by the way Norbett announced his plans that it was going to be another one of those days.

"What sort of plans?" he asked.

"Aha," said Norbett mysteriously. "Aha."

"What exactly does 'Aha' mean?" Bamber had on his Worried Face look.

"Aha," Norbett replied innocently, "means nothing more than 'Aha', that's all."

"Well I don't like the way you say 'Aha'," complained Bamber.

"Bamber," said Norbett in a very matter-of-fact-type voice, "have you ever tried flying?"

"Flying?" exclaimed Bamber in astonishment.

"Yes . . . flying," replied Norbett casually. "You know . . . up in the air."

Bamber's mouth opened and did not close.

"Bamber," snapped Norbett, "would you ever close that mouth of yours. You look as if you're trying to catch flies!"

Bamber closed his mouth very slowly and put on his Hurt Face.

"Now," continued Norbett, "as I was saying, have you ever tried flying in the air?"

"No," growled Bamber, still pouting.

"Well," said Norbett very casually, and as if this was the most natural thing in the world to be asking, "I want you to fly around the forest carrying a long banner behind you."

That was just the way he said it, very matter-of-fact like.

"Fly around the forest?" Bamber spluttered in disbelief.

"That's the general idea," replied Norbett casually, pretending to inspect his paws.

"Do you see these arms?" growled Bamber, his face red and angry looking.

"Do you happen to mean those two things hanging from your shoulders?" asked Norbett, barely looking up.

"Yes!" snapped Bamber. "These are not wings. They are meant to keep me firmly on the ground and are certainly not meant to keep me up in the air."

"Now Bamber," said Norbett soothingly. "Don't be a spoilsport. Admit it . . . you've just never tried to fly."

"BEARS DON'T FLY!" roared Bamber so loudly that some birds sitting in a nearby tree flew off, squawking in alarm.

"Of course they do," replied Norbett gently and he placed a comforting paw around Bamber's shoulder. "You've just never looked to see if there were bears flying around. For all you know the air could be full of flying bears only you never look for them."

Bamber looked up and scanned the skies. "No sign of any at the moment," he growled.

"Now Bamber," said Norbett reassuringly, "you have got to believe in yourself. If you believe you can fly then you will fly. It's a case of mind over matter."

"I don't believe I can fly," said Bamber firmly.

"You must try," said Norbett gently.

"No," said Bamber.

"Yes," said Norbett.

"Never," said Bamber.

"Now," said Norbett.

"*Now?*" squeaked Bamber, backing away.

"Now," said Norbett, following after.

"No," said Bamber, firmly.

"This minute," said Norbett, and he grabbed Bamber. "Now be a good bear and do exactly as I say." He marched the protesting Bamber into his cave and tied a long cloth banner around his neck. Then he marched him back outside again towards a tall tree at the edge of the clearing.

"This won't work!" wailed Bamber.

"Oh yes it will!" Norbett shouted back.

"Oh no it won't!" whimpered Bamber again.

"Yes it will!" shouted Norbett.

"Won't!"

"Will!"

"Won't!"

"Will!"

"Won't!"

"Won't!"

"Will! . . . Will?" Bamber suddenly found himself agreeing with Norbett.

"Attaboy, Bamber," said Norbett triumphantly. "I knew you would come round to my way of thinking!"

"You tricked me!" protested Bamber.

"Nonsense," growled Norbett as he unfurled the cloth, "you just began to believe in yourself."

"I did not," muttered Bamber under his breath.

"Now first of all," interrupted Norbett, "we will have a little training exercise."

Bamber groaned. "Not another training exercise," he said.

"I want you to run along the clearing as fast as you can," said Norbett, all enthusiastic, "and flap your arms up and down in the air as you run."

Bamber gave him a withering look.

"Then, as you are gathering speed start squawking – just like you hear the birds do!"

"Why?" asked Bamber miserably.

"Because we want an air of authenticity, that's why," growled Norbett.

"What's 'authenticity' mean?" asked Bamber.

"I haven't a clue," replied Norbett carelessly. "But it's a big long word and doctors love using big long words so you had better get used to them. I won't know what they all mean. I'll bet they don't even know what they mean. But it doesn't stop them using them."

"Oh," said Bamber. But he didn't really understand.

"Now let's start the first run," ordered Norbett.

Bamber began to jog limply around the clearing.

"Faster, Bamber, faster! Put your heart into it!" shouted Norbett.

Bamber grunted a reply of sorts and gathered speed.

"Squawk!" ordered Norbett as soon as he felt Bamber had reached the correct speed. He followed after, unfurling the banner which had writing clearly marked in red paint:

FOREST MEDICAL CENTRE
Just Opened – Expert Medical Advice
Highly Qualified Staff Available
No Job Too Small – Don't Delay,
Come Today

Bamber started squawking as he ran and began to flap his arms up and down, hoping desperately that he might actually take off.

"Attaboy, Bamber, attaboy!" shouted Norbett encouragingly. "You're a natural!"

Bamber was beginning to believe in himself. He ran faster and faster, squawking all the time, flapping his arms up and down and taking little jumps into the air. Norbett was delighted and roared encouragment all the way.

Eventually Bamber stopped for a rest and sat down on the grass, puffing and panting. "There! I told you so," he grunted, trying to catch his breath. "I said I couldn't fly and I was right. Bears just don't fly. It's as simple as that."

But Norbett wasn't really listening. He was staring at the banner, deep in thought.

"Bamber," he said slowly. "I have a different idea."

Bamber groaned.

"Now," began Norbett, "you take one end of the banner and I am going to take the other end. We'll stretch it out fully until everyone can see the words clearly. Then we'll run together as fast as we can."

"Righto," agreed Bamber eagerly. This sounded all right to him.

"Once we gather enough speed I want you to go 'Nee-Naw, Nee-Naw, Nee-Naw'."

Bamber's mouth opened and closed. "You want me to go what?" he exclaimed.

"Nee-Naw, Nee-Naw, Nee-Naw. You know, just like an ambulance."

"I'm a *bear*," screamed Bamber. "I am not an ambulance!" He wiped a paw

Eventually Bamber stopped for a rest . . .

across his brow, muttering under his breath.

"Now Bamber," continued Norbett soothingly. "If we are going to do this doctor bit properly we are going to have to act the part. What sort of a medical centre will we have if we don't have ambulance noises to go with it?"

Bamber gave Norbett a withering look.

"Now let's try this together."

Bamber and Norbett held the banner stretched out between them until it was taut.

"Nee-Naw, Nee-Naw," started Norbett at the top of his voice, nodding at Bamber to follow.

"Nee-Naw, Nee-Naw," Bamber began and before long the whole forest echoed to the sound of Norbett and Bamber's ambulance noises.

"Okay," shouted Norbett at last, "run!"

Out through the forest they ran as fast as their legs would carry. "Nee-Naw, Nee-Naw, Nee-Naw."

Further ahead a lone fox was having a

midday snooze beside a rock. Into his dreams drifted ambulance noises, all the time coming closer. "Nee-Naw, Nee -Naw, Nee-Naw."

Unfortunately for the poor fox, he woke up at the wrong moment, just as Norbett and Bamber were right behind him.

"Nee-Naw, Nee-Naw, Nee-Naw," rushed into his ears and he stood up suddenly to see what was happening.

"Whooommpphh!" the banner caught him between the eyes and he was engulfed in cloth.

Norbett and Bamber continued running, unaware of what had happened. "Nee-Naw, Nee-Naw, Nee-Naw."

Unluckily for them both, and especially for the fox caught up in their banner, they ran on either side of a large oak tree.

CRASH! went the fox into the tree.

"Aaagh!" went Norbett and Bamber bears as they were suddenly pulled together at the speed of light, still clutching the banner.

"Get out of my way!" they both

shouted as they saw the whites of the other's startled eyes rush towards each other.

CRASH!

The "Nee-Naws" stopped suddenly.

Norbett picked himself up first and then lifted Bamber to his feet. "Dumbo!" growled Norbett angrily.

"Who's a dumbo?" protested Bamber. "You ran into me." They were just about to have an argument when groans and moans from behind the oak tree interrupted them.

Norbett looked at Bamber, eyebrows raised. Bamber shrugged. They both crept slowly over to find the fox struggling desperately to unravel himself from the banner.

Slowly his head appeared and glazed eyes stared up at the sky. "Ouch!" he winced as he massaged his head, trying desperately to figure out what he was doing lying there. "Why does my back hurt so?" he thought. "And my head . . . and my arms and legs . . . I feel as if I've been hit by a tree-trunk."

"Quick Bamber," whispered Norbett, "help me. We've got our first patient."

Bamber and Norbett gently lifted the fox on to the banner and used it as a stretcher.

"You poor fox," said Norbett in his most caring voice. "What happened to you?"

The fox looked at Norbett, then at Bamber. He tried to speak but nothing came out.

"You're very lucky we were nearby," continued Norbett, "and so close to our medical centre. We had better render some first-aid."

Norbett and Bamber carried the fox on their banner-stretcher back to the cave where he was bandaged and strapped and gently nursed back to his feet. He couldn't say enough for the care and attention lavished so generously on him. "But what happened?" he kept asking, "did you see anything?" Norbett and Bamber just shook their heads.

"I seem to remember having a snooze," continued the fox, shaking his head and trying desperately to recall the events. "Then I thought I heard some sort of strange noises . . . something like a 'Nee-Naw' sound. Next thing I woke up lying underneath a tree and aching all over. I just can't make it out at all."

"Strange things do happen in this forest from time to time," said Norbett solemnly, and he looked to Bamber.

"Oh indeed," agreed Bamber quickly. "Some very strange things indeed."

"Well I'd better be off," muttered the fox as he limped towards the door. "You don't by any chance have anything for loss of memory, do you?" he asked.

"Wait one moment," said Norbett and he disappeared to the back of the cave, returning with a bottle of green medicine. "Take this three times every day," he ordered. "Your memory should come back soon."

"Oh thank you, thank you," said the fox as he examined the bottle. He unscrewed the top, took a quick swig and pulled a most unpleasant face. Stopping at the front door for a moment he looked very carefully all around before venturing outside. "Thank you again," he said as he hobbled through the clearing. "I'll be sure to tell all my friends what an excellent doctor and assistant there are here." Clutching the bottle of medicine tightly in his paws he disappeared amongst the trees.

"Now Bamber," said Norbett as soon as the fox was out of sight, "that wasn't exactly a resounding success, was it?"

"I did my best," sniffed Bamber, pouting.

"Your best indeed, Bamber bear," said Norbett. "But we can't go on bashing our patients and then offering to treat them!"

"I didn't bash him," complained Bamber. "Anyway, I nearly killed myself with that madcap scheme of yours." He put on his Hurt Face and retired to the back of the cave to nurse his bruises.

Norbett wasn't listening. He stood at the window, staring outside, deep in thought.

4

Norbett and the Miraculous Cure

Bamber sulked. Norbett pondered. They took a break in the cave and had a light lunch, much lighter than Bamber would have preferred and he promised himself a decent bite to eat as soon as he escaped from Norbett's clutches.

Norbett suddenly stood up and walked back over to the window again, smiling to himself. He looked out for a while, saying nothing, but grinning from ear to ear.

Bamber watched suspiciously. This was Norbett Bear at his most dangerous – plotting and planning!

"Bamber," said Norbett suddenly as he

turned around. He put both paws behind his braces and twanged them against his chest.

Bamber groaned inwardly.

"Bamber, my faithful First Assistant . . . " continued Norbett, his eyes twinkling with mischief. "How good an actor are you?"

Bamber groaned outwardly. "What do you mean?" he asked, not really looking forward to the reply.

"Well," said Norbett, "I have sort of a little plan that involves you."

Bamber's heart sank. First assisting was turning out to be a much more troublesome job than he could ever have imagined.

"What sort of a little plan?" he asked.
So Norbett told him. Bamber gasped. Norbett told him some more. Bamber swooned. Norbett laughed heartily when he had finished. Bamber looked pale.

"Never!" he said most emphatically. "Never, never, never, never!"

"This afternoon," said Norbett firmly.

"Never!" roared Bamber, "N-E-V-E-R. Never!"

"As soon as you're ready," said Norbett and he held up the First Assistant uniform. "You wouldn't like to lose this now, would you, Bamber?"

"That's bribery!" Bamber pointed out.

"Exactly," said Norbett.

Bamber groaned and groaned. He protested and protested.

Norbett ignored and ignored.

Finally the still-protesting Bamber and Norbett left the cave, and went out through the clearing, deep into the forest.

Now every Saturday – and this was a Saturday – at midday all the animals gathered beside a lake in the middle of the forest. This was their weekly get-together and an important day for all of them.

Norbett and Bamber crept very quietly up to the gathering and waited until most of the animals had arrived. Mice were arguing with badgers and horses were arguing with wild cats and they in turn argued with the stray dogs. It was much the same as any other week. Once or twice a passing sheep would butt in or a hedgehog would raise a point of order, but all in all it was very much as you would expect when a group of different animals gather together in any one spot at any one time.

"This won't work!" whispered Bamber as he looked on from behind some bushes.

"You must have faith," growled Norbett.

Bamber groaned.

"Now, Bamber," said Norbett. "You know what you must do. Go to it!" and he pushed Bamber out from the bushes towards the group.

"Hi, Bamber," said one of the sheep, recognising him from a previous meeting.

"Hi, sheep," replied Bamber weakly. He smiled at one or two of the other animals and made his way slowly into the middle. One by one the animals said their "hellos" to Bamber and he did his best to pretend that this was no different to any other

Suddenly he clasped his chest and
started to moan . . .

time. He nodded to each one as they spoke and waved nervously at others too far away to talk with.

Suddenly he clasped his chest and started to moan. "AHHH" he went. "AAGGHH . . . OHHH . . . AHHH. . . OOUUCCHH . . . AAARRRRGGGHHHH! HELP!"

The animals stopped what they were doing and stopped what they were saying to look.

"AAGGHH . . . OOUUCCHH!" cried Bamber again, dropping to the ground and writhing as if in pain. "AHHH . . . OOOOHH . . . HELP . . . OOUUCCHH!"

"What's wrong?" shouted a sheep at last, and they all gathered around Bamber.

"OOOOHHHH . . ." moaned Bamber, rolling on the ground. "GET ME A DOCTOR!"

"Get him a doctor!" shouted the sheep and the others took up the call. "Get him a doctor – he's dying!" they bellowed in confusion. "Give him air!" someone ordered. "Loosen his trousers!" suggested another. "Pinch his nose!" shouted a

mouse and when everyone looked to see who had said this he blushed and ran home as fast as he could.

"Stand back . . . *I'm* a doctor!" came a roar from the bushes. "Let me through!" Norbett strode firmly into the midst of the group. "What seems to be the matter?" he asked.

Bamber started to groan again. "OOOHHHH . . . HELP . . . QUICKLY . . . "

All the animals began to chatter at once. "He's dying . . . he's had a heart attack . . . he's croaked it . . . he's collapsed," they shouted.

"QUIET!" ordered Norbett at the top of

his voice. "Quiet all of you!" He held up a paw for silence. "Stand well back . . . give me plenty of space. This calls for a clear head."

The animals moved back, muttering to themselves and looking on anxiously. A hedgehog said how he had only seen Bamber the day before and how well he had looked and what could possibly have happened to make him sick so suddenly?

One of the cats thought he had been eating too much recently and really shouldn't have been carrying so much weight and that it surely must have strained his heart.

The sheep nodded in agreement when they heard this, as all sheep do, and then agreed with the next speaker . . . and the next . . . and the next.

"Groan you silly bear!" hissed Norbett into Bamber's ear as he knelt down and pretended to examine him. "Put a bit of life into those pains."

"WAIL . . . MOAN . . . GROAN!" went Bamber suddenly and the animals clutched each other with fright.

"Do something!" shouted one of the stray dogs and the others took up his cry. "Yes, do something . . . he's dying . . . help him!" they shouted.

Norbett held up a paw for silence again. "This is a very difficult case," he announced solemnly. "A very difficult case indeed. I will need all my skills to save our bear friend here from total extinction."

The animals gasped. One of the sheep fainted and two of his friends decided to do the same. The hedgehog covered his eyes, which was a bit silly really, as he couldn't see anything anyway from where he stood.

Bamber let out another blood-curdling groan. "AHHH . . . OOOHHH . . . "

"Attaboy Bamber," whispered Norbett, "give them all you've got."

"HELP ME . . . GET A DOCTOR," he struggled to say.

"Don't worry," said Norbett out loud, "you're in safe hands with me. I am a doctor."

"I won't just have anyone . . . "
moaned Bamber, and he rolled around the
ground for greater effect. "I won't have
anyone other than Dr Norbett Bear, MD . . . "
he gasped.

"It is I," announced Norbett triumphantly.
"I am that Dr Norbett Bear . . . er . . . MD!"

"Oh thank goodness," whispered
Bamber through clenched teeth, but loud
enough to be heard.

Norbett stood up and addressed the
group. They were totally silent, clinging to
each other. "This bear," he announced
solemnly, "is in the final throes of a most
dangerous condition called *Acidoluxatus
Cantankerous*."

"Aci-what?" chorused the animals.

"Acido . . . acido . . . acido . . . " Norbett
stumbled over the words. "I will not
repeat myself," he said quickly. "We are
only wasting time. I must give him an
immediate antidote."

"A what?" asked the animals in unison,
and another sheep fainted.

"A what?" asked Bamber under his

breath. "You're going to give me a what?"

"A thick ear," Norbett hissed back, "if you don't lie down there and start moaning."

"I want to know what this anti-something or other is before you give it to me," growled Bamber and he tried to clamber to his feet.

Norbett grabbed his shoulders and pushed him back on to the ground. Bamber struggled. Norbett held firm. "He's going into the last stages," Norbett announced. "They always struggle fiercely before they die!"

Another sheep fainted.

"I will have to use the antidote immediately," shouted Norbett.

"You will not," grunted Bamber through clenched teeth. "Not till I see what it is."

Norbett reached a paw into his pocket and pretended to struggle with something inside. "I AM NOW GOING TO ADMINISTER THE ANTIDOTE," he roared to the group.

All the sheep suddenly recovered and stood up to see what was going on.

Norbett suddenly produced a rubber snake from his pocket and waved it in front of Bamber's nose. "Hiss!" he went. "Hiss!"

Bamber took one look at the snake and sprang to his feet roaring. "Aaaaggghhh . . . heeelllppp . . . aaaggghhh!"

"Hiss!" went Norbett again. "Hiss!"

Bamber let out another roar and all the sheep fainted together. The hedgehog uncovered his eyes in time to see everything, then he too swooned. The wild cats climbed up the trees, the stray dogs jumped on to the horses' backs and the horses hid behind the bushes. Birds flew away and caterpillars stopped caterpillaring.

"Don't worry!" boomed Norbett. "He is all right! The antidote has worked! He has been saved!"

Bamber didn't hear this announcement of his remarkable cure, he was deep in the forest, hiding behind a tree, teeth chattering, looking around wildly to see if the snake had followed.

The animals scattered to the four corners of the forest, bursting to tell their friends and neighbours about all they had seen and heard. As each told the story little bits were added on and other bits exaggerated so that the final tale sounded nothing like what had happened at all. But Norbett had made his mark. The word was out. A new and miraculous healer was present in the forest with powers and medicines never before witnessed.

Bamber refused to come out from

behind the tree when Norbett went to congratulate him on his performance.

"That was a mean and dirty trick you pulled on me," he growled angrily.

"Nonsense," replied Norbett. "That wasn't a real snake – it was made of plastic!" He waved the plastic snake up and down. Bamber groaned and slumped to the ground.

"Anyway we needed a bit of drama. You were superb. Those animals were convinced that you'd been rescued from some terrible illness. I'll bet they are even now queuing up at our medical centre for help. Think of the business you have generated today!"

Bamber wasn't easily consoled and he pulled a few faces behind Norbett's back before making his way back to his own cave. He cooked himself the biggest meal he had ever eaten and collapsed into bed exhausted.

Back at his own cave Norbett was already having to deal with a steady trickle of animals, anxious to meet the miracle doctor.

"Come tomorrow," he told them. "I am exhausted after today's work. Come back tomorrow . . . I will have my assistant then to help."

When they had all finally left Norbett let out a roar. "Attaboy, Bamber! Attaboy! You really wowed them today! Tomorrow we take on the world!"

5

Bamber's First-Cousin-Once-Removed

The next day came and went but Bamber Bear did not report for duty at the Forest Medical Clinic. Neither did he on the following morning or even the day after. Norbett was at his wit's end wondering what to do. The forest was still buzzing with the story of his remarkable healing skills and powers. Each morning brought new patients clamouring at the cave door looking for help. There were hedgehogs with dandruff, horses with colic, cats with mange, scurfy dogs, blind bats, loopy owls and spindly spiders. All were expecting instant cures, just like they heard had happened to Bamber.

Norbett could not control the numbers and their demands.

"I need my faithful First Assistant," he thought at the end of the third day as he lay exhausted, slumped over the table in the middle of his cave. "Where is he? What has happened to him? He couldn't still be sulking, could he?"

Next morning, before the sick and wounded of the forest could gather, Norbett set out to look for Bamber.

Inside his own cave Bamber Bear was relaxing after a hearty breakfast. He had enjoyed his few days of peace and quiet, far away from the demands of flying and feigning ailments. Life was beginning to return to normal.

"Bang, bang, bang, bang!" Someone was hammering on his cave door.

"Are you in there, Bamber Bear?" It was Norbett.

Bamber said nothing.

The letterbox slowly opened and

Norbett's eyes squinted through from the other side. "Bamber . . . are you in?" he growled again.

"No," squeaked Bamber.

Norbett stood back from the door in surprise. Then the letterbox opened again.

"Well who's that in there if it's not Bamber Bear?"

"It's his first-cousin-once-removed," squeaked Bamber again, trying to sound like what he thought a first-cousin-once-removed might be like.

Norbett thought this over for a moment. "I didn't know Bamber had a first-cousin-once-removed," he said.

"Neither did he," replied Bamber carefully, "and he was so surprised when I called to visit that he went straight out."

"Out where?" asked Norbett.

"Out and about," said Bamber.

"Out and about where?" growled Norbett, trying all the time to see who was speaking.

"Out and about wherever he goes when he's out and about," replied Bamber.

Norbett straightened up and stood back from the door, deep in thought. He paced up and down for a moment, his brow furrowed. "That's a great pity," he said finally.

"What's a great pity?" asked Bamber cautiously.

"It's a great pity that Bamber Bear has gone out and about and that you don't know where he is," replied Norbett, peering through the letterbox again.

"Why's that?" asked Bamber, all interested.

"Because I have brought a large cream

cake with me to make up for all the trouble I caused him recently. But if he's not here I shall have to eat it all myself," said Norbett and he made loud chomping noises as if starting into a cake.

The cave door burst open and Bamber stood there looking surprised.

"Norbett Bear!" he exclaimed. "How nice to see you! And what a surprise!" His eyes twinkled mischieviously. "I have just this moment returned after being out."

"Where's your first-cousin-once-removed?" asked Norbett, looking over Bamber's shoulder to the inside of the cave.

"Gone," replied Bamber casually.

"Gone where?" growled Norbett.

"Out and about," replied Bamber.

"Out and about where?" asked Norbett.

"Out and about where first-cousins-once-removed go when they are out and about," replied Bamber, all the time trying to see what was in Norbett's paws. "Where's the cream cake?" he asked.

"Gone," said Norbett.

"Gone where?" asked Bamber suspiciously.

"Out and about," replied Norbett, still craning his neck to see further into the cave.

"Out and about where?" growled Bamber, moving his head to block Norbett's view.

"Out and about where cream cakes go when they are out and about," said Norbett, smirking.

Bamber looked at Norbett and Norbett stared straight back. "You're telling me a pork-pie," accused Bamber.

"No!" exclaimed Norbett loudly. "You are the one telling pork-pies. You and your first-cousin-once-removed!" he snorted. "Humph."

"Well what about your cream cake?" complained Bamber.

"Never mind about that," said Norbett. "Why are you not helping me at the Medical Centre?"

"Because I'm tired of being knocked about," replied Bamber, putting on his

Hurt Face. "I'm tired of running around and nearly breaking my neck. I'm especially tired of the training exercises. And I'm tired of being called a First Assistant and never getting to do any real first assisting." He looked down at the ground, scuffing the grass with his foot.

"All that's over," said Norbett gently and he placed a reassuring paw on Bamber's shoulder. "We don't need any more training exercises. We don't need to climb trees or put on any more acts. The news is all over the forest – I cannot cope with the demand. The place is overrun with sick animals."

Bamber sulked and said nothing.

"Why only yesterday I had a whole family of Dalmatians in," continued Norbett, trying to win Bamber over. "You should have seen them. What a bunch!"

Bamber couldn't resist listening. "What happened?" he asked.

"Wait for it, Bamber, just wait for it. You're never going to believe it!" exclaimed Norbett.

"What did they want?" pressed Bamber.

"You'll never believe this," continued Norbett, shaking his head in disbelief. "In fact I couldn't believe it myself when they started."

"What did they want? Come on, tell me!" cried Bamber. "What were they in for?"

"Well . . . " began Norbett slowly, dragging the story out for better effect. "All six of them piled into the cave together. They lay all over the place and when the last one had settled the oldest dog stands up and says, 'We've come out in spots.' Spots! . . . SPOTS!" Norbett's voice rose higher and higher. "Would you believe it? Dalmatians complaining they had come out in spots!"

"I don't believe it!" said Bamber and he shook his head. "And what did you say?"

"'Spots!' I said," said Norbett. "'SPOTS! . . . What do you think you're supposed to come out in – you're Dalmatians! You're supposed to come out in spots! If you didn't come out in spots you wouldn't be called Dalmatians would you?' I said. 'You might be cocker spaniels or labradors or hyenas or dingos . . . you might be anything else but you wouldn't be Dalmatians!' I said," ended Norbett.

"I don't believe you!" said Bamber. "What a bunch."

"Right on, Bamber," said Norbett. "What a bunch indeed."

"So what did you tell them?" asked Bamber.

"I told them that if they didn't get out of the place as soon as possible I would paint them with stripes and call them zebras. That soon shifted them, I can tell you!"

Bamber grinned. He could just imagine the Dalmatians coming in covered in spots to see Norbett and going out looking like zebras. He chuckled heartily and wished he was back first assisting again, involved in all the fun.

"So now can you see," continued Norbett, interrupting Bamber's thoughts, "now can you see how important you are to me? Now can you see how much I need you back at the Medical Centre? We're a team, you and me. Bamber and Norbett bears – medical supremos!"

"Okay, but no more training exercises," warned Bamber.

"None," agreed Norbett.

"Or acting like ambulances around the forest?" added Bamber.

"Never," said Norbett. "From now on we're a team. In the thick of everything together. Like sugar and spice. Like salt and pepper. Like strawberries and cream."

Bamber sniffed and looked Norbett up

and down. "More like chalk and cheese," he thought. "Do I get to wear my First Assistant uniform again?" he asked.

"I've brought it with me," said Norbett, grinning.

So Bamber and Norbett made up their differences and returned to the clinic where already a long queue of sick and weary animals had gathered, waiting impatiently for Dr Norbett Bear, MD.

6

Norbett Introduces Some Unusual Treatments

Bamber got to work immediately, organising the crowd and making up the medicines that Norbett ordered. He mixed spring water with various herbs to produce a range of different-coloured potions and these were handed out as needed. There didn't seem to be any real pattern to the way Norbett dispensed these, as he sometimes told the patients to drink the liquids or then again he might tell them to rub them on to their legs or paws or wherever they had a rash or felt a pain.

One way or another, Bamber felt that at last he was being useful and actually first assisting. He took great pride in showing each patient into Norbett's cave and standing them in front of the table in the middle of the cave.

A pig turned up with a sore throat. "Can I see the doctor?" he asked Bamber.

"Certainly," said Bamber and he led him into the cave. "Pig with a sore throat," he announced and Norbett marched over to the pig, looking him up and down.

"Say 'Ah'," said Norbett.

"Oink!" went the pig.

"No," said Norbett, "I said say 'Ah'."

"Oink," went the pig again.

"Look," growled Norbett in frustration. "I want you to say 'AH'. Get it? 'AH'."

"OOOIIINNNKKK!" replied the pig defiantly.

Norbett looked as if he would blow a fuse.

Bamber decided this was a good time to first assist. "A word in your ear, doctor, if I may," he said. Bamber proceeded to whisper something into Norbett's ear.

"Good idea, First Assistant, good idea," said Norbett as he listened. "Well worth a try." He turned back to the pig.

"Say 'Oink'."

"Aaaahh!" went the pig.

Norbett smiled at Bamber and Bamber nodded back.

"You have bruised the inside of your throat, pig. What have you been eating?" asked Norbett.

The pig snuffled in embarrassment, blushed, and then told them his daily diet: carrot scraps, cabbage leftovers, apple cores, orange peels, squashed grapes, crushed turnip, banana skins and onion rings. All washed down with sour milk. Bamber began to feel a bit queasy as he listened and Norbett broke into a cold sweat.

"That was breakfast," grunted the pig. "For lunch I had . . . "

"That's enough . . . that's quite enough to be going on with," interrupted Norbett and he sat down at the table in the middle of the cave, shaking his head and mopping his brow.

"Do you know what I think, doctor?" asked Bamber.

"What's that, First Assistant? What do you think?"

"I think," whispered Bamber behind a paw. "I think he's made a right pig of himself, ha, ha, ha! He's made a right pig of himself! What do you think of that?"

The pig looked at Norbett and Norbett looked at the pig. Then they both looked at Bamber. Then Norbett looked at the pig again. The pig raised his eyes to the heavens. Norbett studied the pig closely.

"You might be right, Bamber," he muttered under his breath. "You might just be right."

"What about my sore throat?" complained the pig. "Can you do anything about my sore throat?"

"Take some red medicine. First Assistant, make up some fresh red medicine for our friend the pig here," he said.

"Right away," replied Bamber and he led the pig outside. When he returned he whispered to Norbett. "We used that same red medicine to help a badger with hair loss."

"Did we?" exclaimed Norbett. "What a surprise! Well, at least if we don't clear up his throat, he won't go bald!"

Bamber swooned.

The next patients were a very worried couple of bulldogs and their miserable-looking son. "He can't bark, doctor," piped up Mrs Bulldog when they had gathered in front of Norbett.

"Yes," added Mr Bulldog sadly, "we've got a barkless son."

"It all happened," continued Mrs Bulldog, suddenly looking angry, "after he chased a very wild cat into a corner." She stopped and gave Mr Bulldog a withering look. "Don't interrupt again, Henry. You've caused quite enough trouble already!"

Mr Bulldog raised his eyes to the heavens and muttered something under his breath.

"And stop muttering, Henry. I find it most annoying when you mutter. You're always muttering. Why don't you speak out properly? Is it any wonder poor Walter is the way he is today?" She reached over and gave Walter a lick on the side of his face. Walter smiled back at Mrs Bulldog.

Mr Bulldog looked at Norbett, sighed and shrugged his shoulders. Norbett shrugged his shoulders back at Mr Bulldog. Bamber started to grin but caught sight of Mrs Bulldog glaring at him and quickly stopped.

Norbett opened his mouth to say something but Mrs Bulldog was off again. "He was chasing this perfectly nasty cat around the place and had it cornered when the vicious brute turned on my boy . . . " Mrs Bulldog stopped to wipe a tear from her jowls and gave Walter another motherly lick on his face. "And . . . " continued Mrs Bulldog between sobs, "the brute bit him! Can you imagine? A cat biting my Walter. And a vicious cat at that!"

Norbett murmured something about all cats being vicious brutes and gave Walter an encouraging smile. Walter smiled a feeble smile back.

"He hasn't barked since, doctor," said Mrs Bulldog finally. "My boy has lost his bark."

"A very serious complaint for any dog," commented Norbett.

"A disaster, doctor . . . a disaster for a bulldog!" lamented Mrs Bulldog and she let out a wail that echoed around the cave. Norbett shuddered. Bamber shivered. Mr Bulldog shrugged his shoulders and began muttering into his jowls. Walter smiled at anyone who would smile back. Mrs Bulldog let out another wail.

"Er . . . leave this to us, Mrs Bulldog," suggested Norbett as he watched her square herself up for another roar. "Perhaps if you and your husband stepped outside for a moment, I believe that my faithful First Assistant and myself could sort this little problem out."

"Oh I'd be so grateful," sobbed Mrs Bulldog. "I haven't slept a wink since my boy lost his bark. You don't think he's lacking in something, do you? Maybe he's not getting enough red meat. Or maybe he's sickening for some strange disease. What do you think, doctor? Please help!"

Norbett held up his paw. "Leave it to me, lady. Leave it to me. I think I know exactly what to do."

Mr and Mrs Bulldog shuffled out of the

cave, leaving their precious Walter behind.

Immediately Norbett and Bamber went into a huddle in the corner whispering to one another and throwing furtive glances over their shoulders at Walter. Walter stared at their backs, looking more miserable by the minute. Finally Norbett walked over and said, "Just try a little bark then, Walter. Nothing too strenuous. Just the sort of bark you would give if you saw a mouse."

Walter cleared his throat, summoned up all his strength, threw back his shoulders and croaked. Then he hung his head in shame.

"This calls for a desperate remedy, Bamber," said Norbett. "This calls for a clear head and a horrible face."

"Horrible face?" asked Bamber, puzzled.

"Indeed, a horrible face," said Norbett and he told Bamber his plan. Bamber laughed and Norbett placed a paw over his face. "Ssshhh. Don't let him hear."

"What would Mr and Mrs Bulldog say if they knew?" whispered Bamber. He looked over his shoulder and gave Walter a reassuring smile.

"Nothing," said Norbett. "They are desperate to get young Walter barking again. Think what their neighbours must be saying: 'Oh Mr and Mrs Bulldog, I hear young Walter can't bark properly . . . what a shame . . . I suppose you'll just have to do all his barking for him from now on . . . ' That's what they'll be saying!"

"You're right," agreed Bamber.

Norbett walked over to Walter and placed a friendly paw on his head. "Walter," he said, "why don't you go over there and have a few biscuits?" He turned to Bamber and added, "First Assistant, a selection of best biscuits for our barkless canine friend here."

"Who?" asked Bamber, eyebrows raised.

"For Walter!" hissed Norbett.

"Oh," said Bamber and he went for the biscuits. He returned with a packet which he emptied into a bowl in the middle of the floor.

Walter watched as the biscuits fell out

of the packet and padded over, sniffed and began to nibble. Within moments he was devouring them one by one, his nose buried deep in the bowl.

"One horrible face coming up," whispered Norbett and he crept slowly up behind young Walter. He placed his paws inside his mouth, pulled his lips wide apart and bared his teeth.

"Waagghhh!" he growled as loud as he could into Walter's ear. "Waagghhh!"

Walter looked up sharply, took one look at Norbett and leapt into the air with fright.

Bamber jumped up on the table in the middle of the cave and pulled an equally fierce face. "Waagghhh!" he growled angrily. "Waagghhh!"

Norbett jumped up beside him and the two of them growled down at young Walter.

"Grrrrrr!" went Walter, puffing himself up to his full size. "GROWL! BARK! BARK! GROWL! BARK! GROWL!" he went at the top of his voice and rushed towards Norbett, snapping and snarling. He jumped up and down at the table with a look of pure fury in his eyes, barking and growling.

The door burst open and Mr and Mrs Bulldog rushed into the room, scooping

Walter up in their arms. "He's barking! He's barking!" shouted Mrs Bulldog excitedly. "My boy's barking again."

"And growling," added Mr Bulldog proudly. "He's growling and snarling something beautiful!"

Walter was indeed barking and snarling and growling. If it weren't for his parents' restraining paws he would also have plunged his teeth into Norbett's leg at the edge of the table. Mr and Mrs Bulldog left full of the joys of spring and delighted with their treatment at the Forest Medical Clinic.

"It may not be the way other doctors treat their patients," commented Norbett to Bamber as they climbed down from the table, "but it sure gets results."

Bamber wiped the sweat from his brow and sat down for a rest, his knees still knocking as he remembered Walter's teeth snapping at his ankles. "You're absolutely right, Norbett," he said, "it's not how other doctors treat their patients. But then again, you're no ordinary doctor!"

"Right on, Bamber, right on," said Norbett. "You're absolutely right, I am no ordinary doctor."

The next patient was a hare.

"I think I've got German measles," he announced to Norbett.

"Have you been to Germany?" snapped Norbett.

"No," replied the hare, puzzled.

"Or received a postcard from Germany?"

"No."

"Can you speak German?"

"No."

"Have you ever driven a Volkswagen?"

"What's a Volkswagen?" By now the hare was getting worried at the look on Norbett's face.

"Forget it," growled Norbett. "You haven't got German measles."

"I thought . . . " began the hare.

"What's wrong with ordinary measles anyway?" interrupted Norbett. "Or Irish measles, or good old-fashioned English measles? Now there's a form of measles we don't see too much of nowadays." He turned towards Bamber who nodded in agreement.

"All we seem to hear about is German measles, Hong Kong flu and the like. Nobody seems to want to get sick any more with something simple like mumps. No, it's all this fancy stuff like Mongolian mange or Brazilian bellyache!" Norbett stomped up and down the cave muttering to himself and Bamber made faces to the hare, warning him not to interrupt.

"There's far too much going abroad for holidays and coming back with highfalutin ideas and funny diseases." Norbett moved closer to the hare. The hare backed away. "Have you been out of this forest on strange trips?"

"Nnnn . . . no . . . " stammered the hare, hoping Norbett wouldn't start ranting again.

"Just as well," growled Norbett. "First Assistant!" He looked for Bamber. "A bottle of red medicine for our hoppity hare here."

"But what exactly is wrong with me?" the hare ventured to ask. "Could it be chicken pox?"

"Are you clucking like a chicken?" asked Norbett.

"No," replied the hare.

"Or are you coming out in feathers?" continued Norbett, "or starting to lay eggs?"

"Definitely not!" said the hare firmly. "Definitely no feathers or eggs."

"Well whatever it is, a bottle of red medicine will soon shift it. First Assistant! Bamber, get me another bottle of your best red medicine."

"Coming up," said Bamber and he went out the back to look.

A few minutes later he returned and announced there was no red medicine left.

"Well give him some green medicine," ordered Norbett instead.

"What's with the green medicine, doctor?" asked the hare suspiciously. "How come you order me red medicine and you don't have enough, huh? Next I get offered some green concoction to use – haven't I just seen a mangey sheep with footrot going out the door with the same green gunge?"

Norbett gave the hare a long hard stare.

"That is no ordinary medicine at all," he said. "That has taken years to develop and is made according to a secret formula known only to myself and my faithful First Assistant."

Bamber nodded proudly in agreement.

"What is it then?" asked the hare, examining the bottle closely.

"Hare restorer," said Norbett.

Bamber swooned again.

7

The Most Famous and Important Doctors in the World

Norbett and Bamber were having a well-earned rest when the letter arrived. They didn't notice the envelope sticking out of the letterbox.

"Now Bamber," Norbett was saying. "Let's just run over this again. With some of our patients we may not always want them to know exactly what we are thinking when we discuss their problems. So we have a code of secret phrases. Okay?"

Bamber tried to stop laughing. He was really enjoying himself these days.

Norbett was so busy recently he couldn't deal with all the sick animals on his own. So Bamber Bear FA, previously only a First Assistant, was becoming more and more involved in the doctoring as well. He walked to work each day from his cave, chest puffed out and stomach pulled in, proud as punch.

"What," continued Norbett, grinning from ear to ear, "what exactly do I *really* mean when I say, 'You're a sturdy little fellow'?"

"You're a big fat lump!" shouted Bamber gleefully.

"Correct," said Norbett, grinning. "And what do I *really* mean when I say, 'The doctor is very busy at present'?"

"He's out the back eating a big cream cake," Bamber laughed back.

"Correct!" Norbett stopped to wipe a tear from his eyes. He was also enjoying himself no end. "And what about this one: What medicine do you give a pig with a rash?"

Bamber couldn't speak for laughing.

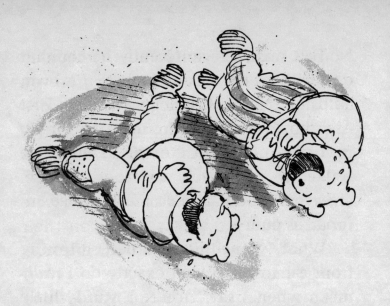

"Come on, Bamber," chuckled Norbett. "What do you give a pig with a rash?"

"I don't know," Bamber could hardly get the words out. "I don't know, what do you give a pig with a rash?"

"Oinkment!" laughed Norbett. "Oinkment. Get it?"

Bamber was doubled over with laughter, the tears streaming down his face. He wiped a paw across his brow.

"What about this," he offered. "Listen to this one."

Norbett blew his nose and wiped a tear from his cheek. "Go on."

"This man," began Bamber, "this man comes to the doctor and he says: 'Can you help me doctor, my dog's got no nose.' And the doctor says, 'How does he smell?' And the man says, 'Awful! He smells awful!'"

By this time Bamber and Norbett were convulsed with laughter, paws on their sides, tears streaming down their cheeks.

"And here's another one."

"Oh no more," cried Norbett, leaning against the table for support. "No more, please."

"It's just a little one," chortled Bamber. "But a good one."

"Go on then," whimpered Norbett.

"What do we *really* mean when we say, 'You don't need any medicine'?"

Norbett thought this over for a moment.

"Don't tell me," he said, holding up a paw. "What do we *really* mean," he puzzled out loud, "when we say, 'You don't need any medicine'?" He furrowed his brow and put on his most Thoughtful

Face. Finally he said, "I give up. What *do* we mean?"

"We haven't got any!" roared Bamber, holding his sides and laughing uncontrollably. "We haven't got any!"

"Oh, good one Bamber," chuckled Norbett. "Good one!"

Bamber suddenly stopped.

"What's that?" he asked, pointing to the envelope.

Norbett followed his gaze and padded over to the door. He picked up the letter, and stared at the writing on the front. Ashen-faced, he turned towards Bamber. "It's from the Outside World!"

Bamber's jaw dropped. "The Outside

World," he whispered. "No one has ever received a letter from the Outside World before!"

Bamber was absolutely right. Their forest was separated from the Outside World, where People lived, by a deep valley through which ran a raging river. The forest animals enjoyed safety and freedom away from humans. They did their best to avoid all contact with the Outside World, as they called it, and stayed well away from the other side. No one before had ever been in direct contact with anyone from beyond the forest. Bamber looked on nervously as Norbett slowly opened the envelope. They exchanged silent glances when he removed the letter and began to read. Bamber had a Worried Look on his face.

Suddenly, Norbett began to smile and chortle. Bamber gave a loud sigh of relief. "What does it say? Come on Norbett, what does it say?"

Norbett held up a paw for silence and read out loud:

From: The Secretary
The Most Famous and
Important Doctors In The World
London
England

Dear Dr Norbett Bear MD,

We have been hearing of your unusual treatments and alternative remedies for illnesses. From what we can gather you and your assistant, Bamber Bear, are achieving a great deal of success with these therapies.

We would like to learn more of your methods and have asked three of our most distinguished Professors to call on you and observe them in detail. They should arrive at the Forest Medical Centre very soon.

Yours sincerely,
Professor MAD Asahatter
(A very smart and important Doctor)

"Fame at last!" roared Norbett and he punched the air with a clenched paw. "Fame at last!"

Bamber was astounded. "They mentioned my name – they know my name!" he whispered.

Norbett danced around the cave,

singing and clicking his claws. Bamber joined him and they held paws to do a Highland fling.

"Knock . . . Knock . . . Knock."

Someone was at the cave door. Norbett padded over and opened up. There stood the three men from the Outside World.

"Good morning," said one. "I am looking for a Dr Norbett Bear."

"MD?" asked Bamber, peering over Norbett's shoulder.

"I beg your pardon?" replied the man, looking puzzled.

"Is it Dr Norbett Bear, MD?" Bamber asked again.

The man studied a piece of paper he held in his hands. "Yes. I do believe you're right," he said. "Dr Norbett Bear, MD . . . "

"Then you've come to the right place," interjected Norbett, holding out a paw. "I am Dr Norbett Bear, MD and this is my faithful First Assistant, Bamber Bear."

"FA," whispered Bamber. "Don't forget the FA bit."

"Er, sorry," added Norbett. "Bamber

Bear, FA."

Bamber smiled and nodded to all three and they in turn nodded and smiled back.

"I am Professor Alphonsus Snob-Value," the first man began again.

"That's your problem," muttered Bamber and Norbett kicked his ankles.

"I am from London, England," he continued. He lifted his hat, revealing an almost bald head, and then introduced the other two. "This is Professor Hans Knees und Bumpsadaisy from Berlin and Professor Ring Tingaling from Beijing."

Professor Tingaling smiled and bowed. "Ah so," he said.

"Ah so what?" asked Bamber and Norbett kicked him again.

Professor Tingaling gave another smile and bow and Norbett smiled and bowed back. Then Bamber smiled and bowed to Professor Bumpsadaisy and Professor Snob-Value. They smiled and bowed and turned towards Norbett to do the same. Before long they were all smiling and bowing to one another and nobody seemed to know where to stop.

Finally Professor Tingaling and Bamber bowed to each other once too often and banged their heads together. Norbett decided that this was as good a time as any to call an end to all the bowing and scraping and ushered the three professors inside.

They sat down at the table in the middle of the cave, looking around and whispering to one another. Finally Professor Snob-Value spoke up.

"Dr Norbett," he said. "We have been

sent by the Society of the Most Important and Famous Doctors in the World. It has come to our attention that you and your assistant," he nodded towards Bamber who put on his Intelligent Face, "are achieving some remarkable cures in these humble surroundings." He paused to look around again and the other two professors did likewise. They shook their heads in amazement.

"We would like to observe you in action," he continued. "If we feel that you are indeed achieving miraculous cures then we will invite you to become a member of our society. You would then be a Famous and Important Doctor – the only bear awarded such an honour."

Professor Bumpsadaisy whispered something and Snob-Value nodded.

"We would also honour your assistant with the title Emeritus Professor of Assistantology."

Bamber puffed his chest out and pulled his stomach in.

"Emeritus Professor of Assistantology,"

he said proudly. "I could live with that."

"Would you excuse us for a moment?" interrupted Norbett and he led Bamber outside. "This is our big chance," he whispered into his ear. "If we impress these three you and I could be the most famous bears in the world."

"I know! I know," muttered Bamber excitedly, eyes glazed at the thought. "Bamber Bear . . . Emeritus Professor of Assistantology. I'd like that."

"Quiet," growled Norbett. "You won't be the Emeritus Professor of anything if we get this wrong!"

"What do you mean?" asked Bamber, pouting.

"We have to impress these people, don't we?" whispered Norbett, looking over his shoulder to make sure he wasn't overheard.

"Yes," agreed Bamber.

"So we'll have to come up with something very special, something really spectacular, right?"

"Right," nodded Bamber, wondering

what Norbett was leading up to.

"So," whispered Norbett, "we need someone very sick and in a lot of pain that I can cure dramatically."

"Yes . . . " agreed Bamber cautiously. This was sounding fine so far.

"So where do we find a sick animal at such short notice?" Norbett stared long and hard at Bamber.

Bamber furrowed his brow and put on his most Thoughtful Face. "I don't know," he whispered. "Do you?"

Norbett said nothing. He just stared at Bamber.

Bamber looked back, puzzled. Norbett kept staring. And staring. Bamber slowly realised what Norbett was plotting.

"No!" he gasped.

"Yes!" Norbett growled back.

"No! You promised!"

"This is the last time."

"You said that the last time!"

"Listen," snorted Norbett, pushing his snout into Bamber's face. "Do you want to be Bamber Bear, plain old First Assistant forever? Or do you want to be Bamber Bear, *superstar*! Bamber, the first ever bear Emeritus Professor of Assistantology?"

Bamber groaned. He knew it was no use protesting any further. "What do I have to do this time?" he sighed. Norbett told him.

"Oh no!" groaned Bamber even louder.

"Quiet!" whispered Norbett, clamping a paw over Bamber's mouth. "Now let's get going before our professors start to wonder what's happening. Remember, bring me one normal patient first. I saw an old sheep and her lamb waiting to see us. They are at the back of the cave. Bring them first. After that we'll spring our surprise." He sauntered jauntily back into the cave with Bamber, muttering under his breath, following behind.

Norbett addressed the professors. "Gentlemen," he began. "My faithful First Assistant and I have been discussing the situation and are quite happy to have you observe us in action."

"Excellent!" exclaimed Professor Snob-

Value.

"I have two patients to show you," continued Norbett. "I believe that the unique way I handle them will impress you no end."

Professor Snob-Value explained this carefully to the other two and they nodded their approval.

"Now," announced Norbett, "my assistant will lead in the first patient." He motioned to Bamber who went outside to find the waiting sheep and her very boisterous lamb. He showed them in and asked the sheep to explain the problem.

"Oh doctor," began the sheep, ignoring the professors. "He has my heart broken. He won't sit still and jumps around the place all day." Sure enough, the lamb suddenly took a leap into the air and landed on top of Professor Tingaling.

"Ah so!" he exclaimed in surprise.

"Ah so yourself," muttered Bamber, and Norbett gave him a withering look.

"See what I mean?" continued the sheep, dabbing her eyes with a handkerchief. "He's like that from morning till night."

The lamb jumped out of Professor Tingaling's lap and knocked a note-pad from Professor Bumpsadaisy's hands. Then he bit Professor Snob-Value's ankle.

"I say!," he cried. "Steady on old chap. Easy on the old nipping, if you don't mind!"

But the lamb ignored everyone. He jumped and leapt around the cave, knocking over chairs and creating an awful racket. The sheep looked on, shaking her head wearily.

"Maybe it's something he's eating," she said hopefully. "Maybe he's allergic to something. Maybe he's one of those hyperactive children you hear about nowadays. Maybe he should be on a special diet."

"Maybe indeed," interrupted Norbett, catching the lamb by the scruff of the neck as he tried to dance past. "Maybe indeed all of those things, Mrs Sheep. However if you leave your frisky young lamb with me for a few moments I'll soon sort him out."

Bamber led Mrs Sheep outside.

"He'll be all right. You'll see a big improvement very soon," he promised.

"Oh I hope so," she sobbed. "I do hope so."

The three professors went into a huddle, watching closely to see how Norbett would handle this difficult case.

Norbett dragged the struggling lamb to the back of the cave and turned him right around so that the watching professors couldn't see exactly what was happening.

He pushed his snout right up against the lamb's face and growled threateningly: "Now my fine young sprite. I've had about as much of your carry-on as I'm going to take. If you don't behave yourself from now on and stop giving your mother a hard time, I will keep you here for a year and feed you nothing but cat food. At the end of that time you won't even know what a bleat is, you'll be meowing so much!"

The lamb suddenly stopped struggling and went ghastly pale.

"And that's just for starters!" growled Norbett angrily. "If that doesn't work I'll get my faithful First Assistant to plaster you with long hair and everyone will think you are a wolf and, boy, will you be in trouble then!" The lamb went completely limp. "After that I will . . . "

"Okay, okay, okay," croaked the lamb. "You win. I'll be good from now on. I was only acting the fool, that's all."

Norbett slowly released his grip, then tightened it again.

"You won't need to be brought back in here again, will you?" he hissed into the lamb's right ear.

"Nnnn . . . nnnooo," squeaked the lamb. "You'll never see me again, I promise you that."

"That's my boy," growled Norbett. "You know it makes sense. Now you walk quietly up to those nice gentlemen from the Outside World, shake each of their hands and tell them how much better you feel already."

The lamb couldn't get out of the place quickly enough. He rushed over to the professors and gave each a hurried handshake.

"I'm cured, I'm cured!" he bleated before disappearing through the door into his mother's grateful arms.

"Wunderbar!" exclaimed Professor Bumpsadaisy, astonished at the dramatic change in the lamb's behaviour.

"Quite extraordinary!" muttered Professor Snob-Value, furiously scribbling notes.

"Ah so!" said Professor Tingaling.

"Vot vas zat method vich you used?" asked Professor Bumpsadaisy.

"Sorry?" went Bamber and Norbett together.

"Vot vas zat method vich you used?" repeated Bumpsadaisy.

Norbett and Bamber exchanged puzzled glances.

"Sorry?" they said again.

"What was that method which you

used?" translated Snob-Value. "Professor Bumpsadaisy comes from Germany," he explained.

"Where they make the measles?" Bamber butted in.

"Sorry?" said Snob-Value, Bumpsadaisy and Tingaling together.

"Nothing," mumbled Bamber.

"Was that a special form of psychology which you used on the lamb?" continued Snob-Value.

"Si who?" asked Norbett, eyebrows raised.

"Psychology," replied the professor. "You know, psychology – understanding the emotional needs of the lamb and employing appropriate rehabilitative procedures."

"Exactly!" said Norbett emphatically. "That's exactly what I did."

"And what do you call this form of psychology?" pressed Snob-Value.

"The Norbett Bear form of child psi-what-ever-you-call-it-ology," replied Norbett.

"Ah so," said Professor Tingaling,

writing everything down carefully.

"Ah so," mimed Bamber behind a paw but stopped as soon as he spotted Norbett glaring at him.

"Now," announced Norbett grandly. Flushed with his immediate success he was anxious to press ahead. "My First Assistant will show in the next patient."

As Bamber walked out of the cave he and Norbett exchanged glances.

Nothing happened for some time and the professors huddled together comparing notes. Norbett pottered around the cave straightening chairs and tidying up.

Then a very feeble knock was heard on the door. Norbett looked up in surprise and listened carefully. After a moment the cave door was tapped again and Norbett walked over to open it.

Outside stood a very old and tatty-looking bear with grey fur around his ears. He was stooped over and leaned heavily on a walking-stick. "Is the doctor in?" asked a weak voice.

"Come in, come in," boomed Norbett. "What can I do for you?"

The old bear hobbled to the centre of the cave and sat down wearily on a chair. He puffed and panted and rested his chin on the walking-stick. The three professors watched silently. Then the old bear sighed deeply and looked around.

"Are you the doctor?" he said to Professor Bumpsadaisy.

"Nein!" replied Bumpsadaisy. "Ze doktor is thar," and he pointed at Norbett.

The old bear shifted in his chair and peered at Norbett.

"Are you the doctor?"

"Yes," replied Norbett. "Dr Norbett Bear, MD at your service."

"What?" said the old bear. "I didn't hear that." He cupped a paw to his right ear. "Are you the doctor?" he croaked again.

Norbett leaned towards the old bear's other ear and shouted, "Yes! I am the doctor." Then he moved slightly so that he stood between him and the professors, blocking their view.

"Great Bamber," he whispered. "You're doing brilliantly! This is your best act ever!" Bamber – for it was indeed Bamber posing as an old bear – just winked and burst into a fit of coughing.

Norbett stood back so that the professors could see everything again.

"WHAT SEEMS TO BE THE MATTER?" he roared into Bamber's ear. Bamber winced.

"WHAT SEEMS TO BE THE MATTER?" he shouted again.

"You're deafening me!" growled Bamber under his breath. "That's what's the matter!" He shifted further back in the chair and moaned for all to hear. "It's my back, doctor. I've had this terrible pain in my back for years and nobody has been able to do anything for me."

"Ah," whispered Professor Bumpsadaisy to Snob-Value. "He hez ze bockity back problem."

"Yes," replied Snob-Value. "And certainly seems to be in a bad way too." He looked at Professor Tingaling. "What

114

do you think?" he asked.

"Ah so," said Tingaling.

"Exactly," agreed Snob-Value.

"Oh, I've been everywhere with my back," began Bamber again, warming to his role. "I've been to faith-healers and bonesetters and vets and horse-doctors and bear-doctors. Nobody . . . " he coughed and spluttered for a moment and groaned loudly. "Nobody has been able to do a thing for me." He leaned back on the chair and let out an unmerciful roar, "HELP ME, DOCTOR! HELP ME! HELP AN OLD BEAR IN DISTRESS!"

Norbett was speechless at the performance and almost clapped. Just in time he collected his wits about him.

"Don't worry, old bear," he said out loud. "You've come to the right place. I am sure I can help."

The three professors watched intently to see what would happen next.

Norbett helped Bamber to his feet. "Take it very easy now, old man. Easy does it."

Bamber grunted and groaned and pulled faces of pain. He shuffled and mumbled, staggered and stumbled, holding on desperately all the while to his stick. Norbett guided him to the table in the centre of the cave and asked him to lay his front paws on the top. Bamber made a great fuss of placing the stick down on the table and becoming a bit unsteady once or twice, gripping Norbett for support.

"You can lay off the theatricals," growled Norbett under his breath. "It's not a talent contest!"

But this only stirred Bamber further.

"OHHH!" he roared. "AAAAA! MY POOR BACK. CAN NO ONE HELP A BEAR IN SUCH TERRIBLE PAIN?"

"Ze poor bere," murmured Professor Bumpsadaisy sadly. "Hees bockity beck ees giving heem such a hard time!"

"Don't worry, old bear," said Norbett loudly. "I'll have you better in no time." He pushed Bamber's head back down and held his shoulders with both paws. "Now where exactly is this pain?"

Bamber threw a paw at the middle of his back and massaged the area. "Here, doctor. Right in this spot."

Norbett placed one paw on the back of his neck and the other on the top of his head. "Have you ever had a very cold sensation in your neck?" he asked out loud.

"No. Never in the neck," replied Bamber.

"Well, you will now," thought Norbett and he pulled out a bag of ice and stuck it against the back of Bamber's neck.

"AAAGHH!" roared Bamber. "AAAGH! MY NECK! EEEEEKKK!"

Norbett just as suddenly burst the bag open, dropping the ice cubes down Bamber's clothes and rubbing them all over his back.

For a split second Bamber didn't move. Then he let out an almighty roar.

"ROAR!" he went. "ROOAARR!" He shot up in the air, leaped across the table, jumped over a chair, vaulted up on to the

117

windowsill and disappeared outside.

Norbett turned to the professors. "Another satisfactory result, if I may say so myself," he said smugly. "That elderly bear could hardly walk in here. After a little careful manipulation he was able to jump out of the window and even now is probably dancing through the forest with joy."

"Wunderbar! Zees ees trulee wunderbar!" exclaimed Professor Bumpsadaisy excitedly.

"Ripping, old chap!" congratulated Snob-Value. "Absolutely ripping! I'm astounded at your treatments. Well done." He shook Norbett's paw.

"Ah so," said Professor Tingaling. "I blouw to sluch powelful heala," and he bowed to Norbett.

Norbett bowed back. "Oh it was really nothing," he claimed modestly. "All in a day's work in here, I'm afraid."

The professors gathered up their belongings and said their goodbyes to Norbett.

"But vere ees your feethful azziztent?" asked Professor Bumpsadaisy at the cave door as they were leaving.

"Afternoon off today," replied Norbett casually. "I'm far too good to him you know. Really for the money I pay that bear, he should put in a bit more time and effort."

The three professors murmured agreement. One by one they shook Norbett's paw and disappeared into the forest. Norbett was just about to shut the door when Professor Snob-Value hurried back, looking furtively over his shoulder.

"You don't by any chance have anything for hair?"

"Hare?" asked Norbett in surprise.

"Yes. Anything to help hair?"

"Well, we have hare restorer," said Norbett. "Would that be what you want?"

"Exactly!" cried Snob-Value gratefully. "That's exactly what I'm looking for . . . hair restorer."

So Norbett fetched a bottle of his best Hare Restorer medicine and gave it to

119

Snob-Value.

"Thank you, thank you very much," he mumbled and immediately rubbed some on to his bald spot.

"Thank you again." Then he disappeared into the forest after his friends.

"What a bunch!" thought Norbett as he watched him go. "Imagine rubbing hare restorer on to your head! And he nearly as bald as a coot. That stuff will lift the bit of hair he's got left!"

He turned around to find a note pinned to the cave door:

DO NOT LOOK UP IF YOU KNOW
WHAT'S GOOD FOR YOU

"Do not look up if I know what's good for me?" Norbett puzzled out loud, looking up.

"KARRRAAAMMMBBBAAA!" came a growly roar from the roof of the cave and Bamber Bear tipped a bucket of icy water on to Norbett's head.

"Agh!" went Norbett.

SPLASH! A second bucket found its target.

"Beware the revenge of the First Assistant!" roared Bamber as he emptied a third. "Ha ha ha . . . hee hee hee . . . ho ho ho!"

Norbett looked up with a rueful grin on his face and Bamber grinned back.

"Attacked!" growled Norbett. "Attacked

by my own First Assistant. What's the world coming to?" His teeth started to chatter and drips formed on his snout. "I could get pneumonia out of this," he muttered. "I wonder should I see a doctor?"

8

Help for a Dragon

Norbett and Bamber soon made up their differences.

Within days, certificates arrived from the Outside World confirming that they had both been honoured by the Society for the Most Important and Famous Doctors in the World.

Norbett was the first ever bear to become a member and Bamber was duly elected Emeritus Professor of Assistantology. While Norbett took it all very calmly, Bamber wandered around the forest telling the news to anyone he met. Many of the animals started to bow every time he came near, pleasing him no end. His chest puffed out with pride and there was an extra lift to his step.

They were in Norbett's cave having a well-earned rest when, suddenly, an almighty crash hit the cave door.

"What was that?" roared Norbett, shaken from a doze.

"I don't know," muttered Bamber and pulled the cave door open to look outside. A large green shape filled the door frame, blocking the light. Suddenly the shape moved back and Bamber looked up.

"EEEEKKK!" he screamed and backed away as fast as he could. "It's a d . . . d . . . d . . . it's a d . . . d . . . d . . . "

"It's a d . . . d . . . d . . . what?" growled Norbett from the comfort of his couch.

"It's a d . . . d . . . d . . . d . . . d . . . " stammered Bamber and he tried to hide behind the door. Norbett clambered wearily from the couch and padded over to look out.

"AAAGGGHHH!" he roared and backed away quickly. "It's a dd . . . dd . . . dd . . . dd . . . "

124

"Exactly," chattered Bamber through clenched teeth. "It's a d . . . d . . . d . . . d!"

Then a very loud, deep and roary voice came from outside. "I'm awfully sorry to bother you, but is the doctor in?"
Dead polite was the voice. Real polite indeed.

Bamber clutched hold of Norbett and Norbett tried to bolt but stood rooted to the spot.

"I hope I'm not calling at an awkward time?" came the voice again. Loud, deep and roary as before but still dead polite.

Bamber and Norbett both poked their heads out the door at the same time and there stood the tallest dragon they had ever dreamed of. Beside him stood another, only slightly smaller dragon.

"Who . . . who . . . who are you?" asked Norbett, trying to untangle himself from Bamber and sound brave at the same time.

"I'm Archibald Bartholomew Cedric Dragon from the next valley," replied the dragon, and he smiled a warm smile. Then he puffed some smoke through his nose as

*"I'm awfully sorry to bother you,
but is the doctor in?"*

if to show he was the real thing. "That's a bit of a mouthful so my friends call me ABCD." A small tongue of fire blew from his mouth as he spoke. "Isn't that a laugh?" he chortled. "ABCD! . . . Ha . . . ha . . . ha . . . he . . . he . . . he!"

"Oh that's a real killer," agreed Norbett weakly. "Ha . . . ha . . . ha . . . he . . . he . . . ho . . . ho . . . That really breaks me up. ABCD . . . ABCD . . . who'd ever have thought . . . " and he looked at Bamber. But Bamber had only heard Norbett say it was a real killer and then passed out! He was lying in a heap at the side of the cave door.

"I say," said the dragon, "is your friend all right? I hope I haven't frightened him or anything? Maybe he's not used to seeing dragons or something?"

"Well as a matter of fact," replied Norbett, trying to lift Bamber up, "he's not that used at all to seeing dragons."

Bamber began to come to, then caught sight of the dragon peering down at him and promptly swooned again.

"Get up out of that," growled Norbett.

Bamber opened his eyes and slowly struggled to his feet. He kept a wary eye on the two dragons and shuffled closer to Norbett for support.

"Haven't you seen a dragon before?" asked the dragon.

"Not around these parts," sniffed Bamber.

"Or any other parts," added Norbett, eyeing the dragons up and down.

"In fact," said Bamber, "we've never seen a dragon before at all!"

"What a pity," sighed the dragon.

"Not if you're a bear," muttered Bamber. "It's no big deal at all!"

"Well we're not all fierce like we're cracked up to be," continued the dragon.

"Oh right . . . convince me," thought Norbett. But he said, "Of course not. I'm sure we only ever hear the bad stories. What takes you to these parts anyway?"

"I have a slight difficulty with Archibald junior here," replied the dragon, still with the deep, roary, polite voice. "And we can find no one to help him at all where we live. We've been to the local Wizard but he seems to know nothing about the problem. Then we heard about Dr Norbett and his First Assistant, Bamber Bear. We thought we might wander over from our valley to see if they could perhaps help."

Norbett drew himself up to his full height. Beside him Bamber began to recover his composure and tried to look businesslike.

"Did you hear that," he muttered to Norbett. "They've heard of Bamber Bear, First Assistant."

"Quiet," muttered Norbett, thinking furiously what to do next. He put on his most doctorish face. "Well now," he began. "I am indeed Dr Norbett Bear, MD and this here," he nodded towards Bamber who by now had a smug grin all over his face, "is my faithful First Assistant, Bamber Bear FA."

Bamber bowed. The dragon reached a scaly claw down and shook Norbett and Bamber's paws.

"Awfully pleased to make your

acquaintances," he said in his real polite, roary voice. "Say hello to the doctor, Arch," he said, turning towards the younger, smaller dragon who let a puff of smoke out through his nostrils. He reached his scaly claw down and shook Norbett and Bamber's paws.

"Awfully pleased to make your acquaintances," he said in a real polite roary voice as well.

These were two dead polite dragons, not a bit like the ferocious sort Norbett and Bamber had read about.

"What seems to be the trouble with young Arch?" asked Norbett boldly, no longer afraid of the dragons.

"Well," began the senior dragon. "Young Arch, as you call him, has lost his fire. He can't breathe fire when he's in the mood. No big flames leap from his mouth when the notion takes him."

Young Arch held his head low with shame and went bright red with embarrassment. Bamber gave him a reassuring smile. He was beginning to like these dragons and felt quite sorry for the young Arch.

"As you can imagine, this causes all sorts of problems over in our valley where dragons are expected to do this sort of thing fairly often," continued the senior dragon.

Norbett murmured in agreement. "Exactly, exactly. I mean what else do dragons do if they can't breathe fire and smoke?" he said.

"Oh, no problem with smoke," interrupted dragon senior. "Plenty of smoke. We breathe bags of the stuff, don't we, Arch?" and he gave dragon junior a playful pat on the head. "Absolutely knee-deep in smoke at times, but no fire. No fire at all, and fire is very important for a dragon to show his spirit."

Then dragon senior threw his head back, puffed a stream of smoke out both nostrils and let forth with an almighty tongue of fire across the clearing. The flames just poured out of his mouth and scorched a tree at the far end where two squirrels were sampling some winter nuts. They suddenly found their backsides on fire and scurried around the tree until the flames died out.

"See what I mean by fire?" asked dragon senior, oblivious to the screeches of the scorched squirrels.

"Indeed," whispered Norbett in awe. "Indeed that's some asset." Bamber said nothing. He stood rooted to the spot, mouth open.

"So it's awfully embarrassing for the whole family to have Archibald junior fireless when he's out playing with his friends," continued dragon senior. "Do you think there's anything at all you could do to help? As I've said, our local Wizard hasn't a clue what to do. He's really quite baffled by the whole thing. Says he hasn't had a case like this ever before."

"A difficult problem," agreed Norbett, "but not impossible for myself and my faithful First Assistant." Bamber was about to protest all ignorance but caught sight of Norbett giving him a withering look. "One moment, First Assistant, if you please. Inside."

Norbett ushered Bamber through the cave door and turned to dragon senior. "Excuse us for the moment," he said. "We need to confer about how best to tackle this situation."

"Oh by all means," said dragon senior. "Take as long as you need. We'll wait outside here until you're ready."

A real couple of polite dragons were Archibald Bartholomew Cedric Dragon and his son Arch junior. Not your usual sort of dragon at all.

"Right, Bamber," began Norbett as soon as he had Bamber in behind the cave door and out of earshot of the dragons. "This is a tough nut to crack but think how our reputations will rise all over the next valley if we crack this one!"

"What do you know about dragons?" whispered Bamber behind a paw, looking out of the door nervously.

"Nothing. Nothing at all, but they can't

133

be any worse to deal with than half the animals that have paraded in front of us these past few days," replied Norbett, all the time plotting his next moves.

His eyes danced in his head as he schemed and Bamber knew only too well not to expect any let-up.

"I know . . . I know!" Norbett exclaimed suddenly. "We'll make up a special potion that should bring back the flames to any dragon. Quickly, follow me." He raced around the cave collecting ingredients. "Get the biggest pot there is," he ordered and Bamber chased after him with an enormous cauldron, the sweat blinding him as he struggled to carry it.

"First we put in two tubes of hot mustard," and Norbett squeezed the whole of the tubes into the pot. "Next we add a whole box of hot chilli peppers, two packets of very hot Madras curry powder and six bottles of horseradish sauce. Now stir that around first." Bamber stirred the mixture with a long-handled spoon and kept his nose well away. "Now we add five bottles of Tabasco sauce, two dozen aniseed balls and twenty spoonfuls of cayenne pepper."

"What else do we need, now?" Norbett pondered.

"A pair of fast running shoes if this plan doesn't work," muttered Bamber under his breath.

"I know . . . I know!" he exclaimed. "Something that is guaranteed to bring out the flames in any dragon who drinks this . . . throw in all our coloured medicines!"

So into the pot went a green liquid to clear worms in cattle. Next came a yellow gunge for dandruff in cats, followed by a blue potion for boils on the backsides of hairy dogs. All the time Bamber looked nervously at the simmering mixture. Then Norbett poured in a horrid-looking gooey mixture he used to get rid of nits from the fur of rabbits. Just when Bamber thought there had been enough, in went a red bottle of fly killer and an orange jelly for lifting warts from the tails of horses.

Bamber could hardly control the cauldron, so hot had it become, and little spits of the mixture shot over the edge every now and then, singeing Bamber's fur.

"Heaven help any dragon who drinks this potion," thought Bamber as he carried the pot outside under the watchful eye of Norbett.

The two dragons watched with deep interest and smoke wafted out of both their nostrils. Every now and then a small flicker of flame licked the edges of dragon senior's lips. Arch junior looked a bit apprehensive as the steaming, foaming potion was placed at his feet.

"Drink all of this down in one go," ordered Norbett, giving the mixture one final stir.

Arch junior looked at his father for support and he nodded in encouragement. "Go on, Arch. Do as the doctor says."

The younger dragon craned his long neck down to the pot and sniffed the mixture. It didn't seem too bad to him at

all. Then with one long "glug . . . glug . . .
glug" he polished off the whole lot and
sat back on his hind legs. Everyone looked
at him expectantly. He licked his lips,
then bent down to lick the last few drops.
He was just straightening up again when
it began to take effect.

"GGGRRROOOWWWLLL!" went Arch
junior and he hopped from one leg to the
other as his face turned all the colours of
the rainbow. "RRROOOAAARRR!" he
went again as the mixture hit his stomach
after the long journey down his throat.
Then he took off around the clearing,

running in circles, roaring and growling at the top of his very loud roary voice. All the politeness seemed to have disappeared. Bamber took to his heels and fled to the safety of the cave but Norbett stood his ground. Dragon senior watched nervously.

"GGGRRROOOWWWLLL!" went Arch junior as he hit a tree-trunk at full speed, knocking out a few teeth and losing scales.

"RRROOOAAARRR!" he roared again. He threw his head fully back on his long neck and let go with a ball of fire from his mouth that almost burned a tree to the ground at the edge of the clearing.

Birds and small animals scattered everywhere and the same two squirrels with the burnt backsides nearly had their whiskers singed off this time. They waved their tiny fists at the dragons before scurrying into a hole in the tree for safety.

"GGRROOWWLLRROOAARR!!" went Arch junior again and he let fly with another ball of fire into the air.

"Hooray!" cheered Norbett and dragon senior together.

"Hooray!" cheered Bamber from the safety of the cave, watching the whole carry-on through the window.

"Oh well done, Arch!" congratulated dragon senior as he watched the younger dragon spout fire and brimstone out of his mouth as often as he wanted. "Well done, Arch, indeed. You've got your fire back again. You're a real fire-breathing dragon again. Well done!"

If truth be told, young Arch felt as if he was totally on fire himself and his tummy sounded like a volcano erupting. Still, he was pleased to be breathing fire again and he put on some real displays to show off and to cool down his red hot insides.

Dragon senior was delighted. He turned to Norbett and shook him warmly by the paw.

"Thank you ever so much, Dr Norbett. I don't know what we would have done without your help."

"Nothing to it, old dragon," replied Norbett. "Nothing to it at all. All in a day's work around these parts."

"No . . . nothing to it," piped in Bamber now that he could see a successful outcome. He strode confidently from the cave. "This is the sort of thing we handle all the time."

He pointed to the notice at the front door.

"No job too small," he read out loud. "This is all in a day's work for Dr Norbett bear, MD and his faithful First Assistant, Bamber Bear, FA."

Norbett gave him a withering look. "Don't overdo it."

Bamber just smiled contentedly.

Arch junior was still trying out his newly-restored flame-throwing skills as the dragons made their way out through the forest and back to their own valley.

"Do come and visit us some time," ABCD shouted back at Norbett and Bamber. "We'd love to see you."

Norbett and Bamber waved goodbye.

"Now there's a couple of real nice dragons," said Bamber as he watched them disappear through the trees.

"Indeed," agreed Norbett. "A couple of dead nice dragons."

They were just about to return to the cave when who should appear in the clearing but the unfortunate fox they had nearly strangled.

"Hello fox," said Bamber.

"Hello bear," replied the fox. "I was wondering if I might have a word with the doctor."

"Certainly," boomed Norbett and he placed a paw around the fox's shoulders. "What can I do for you?"

"Have you any of that memory medicine left?" asked the fox.

Norbett and Bamber exchanged glances.

"Er, what colour would that have been now?" asked Bamber, trying desperately to recall what they had passed off on the fox.

"I can't remember," replied the fox.

"Was it in a big bottle or a small bottle?" Norbett queried.

"I can't remember."

"Did you take all of it?" asked Bamber.

"Did I take all of what?" replied the fox.

"The medicine," snorted Bamber. "Did you take all of it?"

"I can't remember."

Norbett and Bamber exchanged weary glances.

"It's been a big success, then, hasn't it?" said Norbett.

"What has?" asked the fox, looking puzzled.

"THE MEMORY MEDICINE!" roared Norbett.

"Oh yes," said the fox enthusiastically. "It's really great stuff."

"For the memory?" asked Bamber sarcastically.

"No. Not for the memory. For dandruff. I used to be plagued with the stuff. Since I took that memory medicine I can't remember the last time I had dandruff!"

"You can't remember?" muttered

Norbett.

"No," smiled the fox. "Isn't that great?"

"Marvellous," agreed Bamber and he produced a bottle of yellow medicine he had used the day before to cure fleas in a donkey. "Try this."

"Thank you very much," shouted the fox gleefully and he disappeared into the forest as suddenly as he had appeared.

Norbett and Bamber watched him skip through the bushes and trees and exchanged shrugs.

Back in the cave Bamber was making himself the largest jam sandwich he could safely fit on a plate when he noticed Norbett staring at the ceiling, deep in thought. He groaned inwardly, knowing all too well this could only mean trouble.

"Bamber," said Norbett slowly. "I've been thinking." Bamber groaned outwardly. He looked wistfully at the jam sandwich, suddenly not so hungry after all.

"Bamber," continued Norbett, "I've

been thinking a lot."

He paused. Bamber waited, hardly daring to listen.

"Maybe we should open a hospital . . ."

"Aagh!" roared Bamber Bear. "Aagh . . ."

Also by Poolbeg

The King's Story

By

Gaby Ross

When the King of Sandonia is deposed the first thing he has to do is get another job. Not easy when all you know is being a ruler.

He is allowed to stay on in his palace with his daughter, Princess Clara, and they have to learn how to light the fire, make tea, get the central heating going, and where to put the bins.

Clara has to adjust to going to school, which she hates, and the king gets the dole and the runaround.

Things get complicated when thieves break into the castle cellar in search of the Lost Treasure of Sandonia and kidnap the princess. The outcome is unexpected and noisy!

Also by Poolbeg

The Moving Stair

By

Gabriel Fitzmaurice

So I jumped upon it
With a spaceman kind of hop,
And up, up, up I floated
But the stair just wouldn't stop.

The pieces in this delightful collection of
poems by Gabriel Fitmaurice reflect the
excitement, newness, joy and high spirits of
the life of young people. Mums and Dads,
school, new babies, animals, sunshine and
snow – all appear in a totally unexpected way
as if through they eyes of the child.